No Pets Allowed!

AND OTHER ANIMAL STORIES
Compiled by the Editors
of
Highlights for Children

BOYDS MILLS PRESS

Compilation copyright © 1992 by Boyds Mills Press, Inc.
Contents copyright by Highlights for Children, Inc.
All rights reserved
Published by Boyds Mills Press, Inc.
A Highlights Company
910 Church Street
Honesdale, Pennsylvania 18431

Publisher Cataloging-in-Publication Data
Main entry under title.
   No pets allowed : and other animal stories / compiled by the
Editors of Highlights for Children.
   [96] p. : ill. ;   cm.
Stories originally published in Highlights for Children.
Summary: A collection of stories on various animals, including dogs
and cats.
ISBN 1-56397-102-X
[1. Animals—Fiction] I. Highlights for Children. II. Title.
       [F]   1992
Library of Congress Catalog Card Number: 91-77000

Drawings by Judith Hunt
Distributed by St. Martin's Press
Printed in the United States of America
   2 3 4 5 6 7 8 9 10

Highlights® is a registered trademark of Highlights for Children, Inc.

CONTENTS

No Pets Allowed!

By Eileen Spinelli

Henry D. Penrose was a dog with a pedigree. He lived in a fine stone house with white marble steps and red velvet drapes on every window. His owner, Professor Randolph Penrose, was quite rich.

Each morning Henry was driven to Obedience School in a long black limousine. Each afternoon he was fed two grilled lamb chops for lunch. Each evening he fell asleep in his fur-lined basket in front of the fireplace. On Saturdays he was groomed at Miss Fifi's Shop. And on Sundays he accompanied the professor to the park, where a classical orchestra played soothing music and the grass was cool and fragrant.

Professor Penrose would stroke Henry's shiny coat and say, "You have the life, Henry my boy!" And Henry certainly had to agree.

Then one day it all changed, just—like—that. Professor Penrose received a telegram offering him a chance to dig for dinosaur bones in Idaho, for one entire year. There was only one problem. The telegram stated quite firmly in the largest letters possible: NO PETS ALLOWED!

"I'll take Henry to my house," offered Mrs. Washburn, the cook.

"I hate to send you off to live on the other side of the city, Henry. There won't be any marble steps or red velvet drapes at Mrs. Washburn's house," said Professor Penrose.

A sad Henry was buttoned into his red plaid coat and driven by limousine to the Washburn residence. When Henry stepped out of the limousine, he was shocked. Such an untidy home. It was all he could do to maintain a sense of dignity.

He was picking his way through the toys on

the front steps when a tumble of children spilled onto the porch and scooped him up. Each time he tried to run away, little hands grabbed him back.

"Don't be too rough, children," said Mrs. Washburn. "Henry isn't used to such fun."

"Fun? Ha!" barked Henry.

Dinner that evening was a big steamy ham bone. Bits of cabbage fell from it as one of the children tossed it into the old plastic bowl that served as Henry's plate. What? thought Henry. No place mat? He wondered if he'd ever see a grilled lamb chop again.

By bedtime, Henry was exhausted. His fur-lined basket had been left behind. "Where will I sleep?" barked Henry. Two of the children carried him off to a room with three bunk beds.

"Henry's sleeping with me!" announced one child, pulling him to one bunk.

"Oh, no! Henry's sleeping with me!" protested another, yanking him toward another bunk.

A third child elbowed his way in, and Henry flopped to the floor. Before he could crawl under one of the beds, a pillow fight broke out. *Thwack!* A pillow smacked into Henry. "Stop! Stop! Stop!" he barked.

Mrs. Washburn came scurrying down the hallway. The children scattered into their beds. "Why, Henry!" scolded Mrs. Washburn. "You never barked like that before! Quiet down, or the children will never get to sleep!"

On Sunday there was no park or classical orchestra, no cool and fragrant grass—just the Washburns' backyard with its dandelion clumps and creaky swings and a fort made out of empty cardboard boxes. All morning, the children wrestled with Henry. They scratched his ears and tied an old red Christmas ribbon around his neck. They tried to make him chase the cat next door. Baby Washburn even kissed him—a big, sloppy, wet, strawberry-lollipop kiss, right on the nose.

Later, when Baby toppled over onto Henry's tail, they both cried: "Yeeeeoooooooow!"

Mrs. Washburn poked her head out of the back door. "Don't hurt Baby, Henry."

"Humph!" barked Henry.

Days, weeks, months passed. Henry learned to put up with pillow fights and strawberry kisses. He learned to ignore the neighbor's cat and to wriggle Christmas ribbons off his neck. He even learned to eat steamy ham bones out of a plastic bowl.

And then one day everything changed, just—like—that. Professor Penrose returned. The long black limousine came to take Henry back to the professor's fine stone house.

The Washburn children gathered on their front

porch. Tears streamed down their cheeks. "Good-bye, Henry," they sniffled. "Good-bye!"

"Bye-bye," barked Henry, sadly.

That evening, after being groomed by Miss Fifi (who kept sighing over the tangles in his coat) and after being fed two plump, perfectly grilled lamb chops (in his own monogrammed dish with a place mat), Henry climbed into his fur-lined basket in front of the fireplace.

"You have the life, Henry," said Professor Penrose. "Welcome home."

Henry yawned. He laid his head on his front paws. He closed his eyes. But he did not go to sleep. Something was wrong. Everything was so quiet, so peaceful. *Too* quiet. *Too* peaceful. Henry climbed out of his basket. He nudged open the front door and headed down the road. At first he walked properly, as he had been taught. Then he ran.

At last he arrived. He scratched at the door.

Mrs. Washburn opened it. "Why, it's you, Henry. Welcome home!"

"Home!" barked Henry, and he dashed up the stairs and into the children's bedroom. *Thwack!* A pillow smacked him.

"Stop! Stop! Stop!" barked Henry as he ducked under one of the beds. As he drifted off to sleep, he gave a last "Woof!" You have the life, Henry, my boy, he thought. You have the life.

It All Started with the Ant

By Margaret Meacham

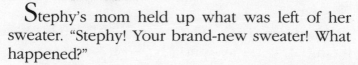

Stephy's mom held up what was left of her sweater. "Stephy! Your brand-new sweater! What happened?"

"It's kind of hard to explain," said Stephy. "I guess it all started with the ant."

"Are you trying to tell me that an ant did this to your sweater?"

"No, Mom. See, the ant was crawling on Sarah Louise's cheek. And when Roddy told her there was an ant on her cheek, she screamed." As she explained, Stephy put the box she was holding on the floor and sat down.

"Mmm hmm," Mom said.

"Well, when Sarah Louise screamed, Mrs. Willis dropped her chalk, and Tommy and Harlow both bent down to pick it up, and they bumped heads."

"Oh, I hope they weren't hurt."

"No. Not really. But Tommy kind of fell backwards, and he knocked over the hamster cage, and all the hamsters got loose."

"Oh, no. All of them?" asked Mom.

"Yup. And they all ran into the coatroom and started eating everyone's lunch. Then Johnny caught two of them, and Sally got one. And I caught two. Know how?"

"How?"

"I threw my sweater on them and trapped them."

"Oh. So that's what happened to your sweater."

"No, Mom. They didn't hurt it at all. After I got them out of it, I just put it back on."

"I'm confused. Stephy, what's in that box?"

"I'll get to that in a minute, Mom. But see, one of the hamsters had eaten part of my sandwich, and Mrs. Willis said I had to throw the whole thing out. She got me some pea soup from the cafeteria, but it was horrible. Yuk. So Sammy gave me half of his peanut butter and jelly sandwich."

"Stephy, I think that box just moved!"

Stephy put her foot on top of the box. "It's okay, Mom. So Sammy said since he gave me half of his sandwich, I had to teach him how to do my flying jump from the playground bike rack. But today my sweater got caught on it."

"So that's what happened to it."

"Well, no. It was okay after that, except for the string that got pulled out of it."

There was a scrabbling sound from the box.

"What was that?" asked Mom.

"Nothing," said Stephy. "But, see, this little string was hanging from my sweater, and when the kitten got the string caught on his claw, he kind of pulled the whole sweater apart. He didn't mean to do it, Mom."

"The kitten?"

"The one that Tommy and I found on our way home."

Mom sighed.

"I told you it was hard to explain, Mom."

"I see what you mean," she said.

More sounds came from the box on the floor.

"Stephy, the box?"

Stephy picked up the box.

"That's what I wanted to talk to you about, Mom." She opened the box and pulled out a furry kitten. "Don't you think it's time we had a cat around here?"

15

Just Like a Hero

By Alan Cliburn

John Henry unfolded the paper and groaned. It was there, all right—right on the front page!

"Come on, John Henry," his mother called. "Your breakfast is ready."

"I'll take the paper," his mother said. "Your breakfast is on the—why, John Henry, whatever is the matter with you? Are you sick?"

"No, I'm okay," John Henry told her. "It's

just—well, look at the front page of the paper."

His mother barely glanced at the picture in the middle of page 1. Then she stared at it. "John Henry, it's you!" she exclaimed. "It's you and Mrs. Pettigrew's cat, Mouser."

John Henry swallowed. "I know."

" 'John Henry Colton, age 10, with a neighbor's cat,' " his mother read, " 'which he rescued from an elm tree on Clark Street yesterday. Hero Colton volunteered to go after the cat when the fire department was unable to send its rescue squad.' "

"I'm not a hero," John Henry muttered.

"You certainly are! I'm going to get an extra copy of this paper to send to your grandmother."

John Henry started to say something but changed his mind. If he told her not to send the paper to Grandma, he'd have to tell her the rest—that it was his fault the cat was up in that tree in the first place.

A few days earlier Mrs. Pettigrew had asked John Henry to take care of Mouser. "I'm going up north to visit my sister," she'd explained.

"But I don't know how to baby-sit a cat," John Henry had started to tell her.

"All you have to do," Mrs. Pettigrew assured him, "is fill her food dish every morning and make sure she has plenty of water."

"Okay," John Henry agreed. "I can do that."

18

"One more thing," added Mrs. Pettigrew. "I don't want Mouser going outside while I'm gone. Make sure you close the screen door when you're fixing her food."

"I'll be careful," John Henry promised.

"This is where I hide the key," Mrs. Pettigrew went on, lifting a flowerpot. "See?"

John Henry nodded.

"And it'll be our secret," Mrs. Pettigrew had said with a wink. "Thank you, John Henry. I know I can trust you."

While he ate breakfast, John Henry thought about Mrs. Pettigrew and Mouser and that picture in the newspaper. If only that photographer hadn't come along just in time to take the dumb old picture.

"John Henry," his mother said suddenly. "Guess who just called—Mrs. Simpson of the Pet Lovers Club. The Pet Lovers want to present you with a special award for rescuing Mouser. 'It's not every day that we have a hero in our midst'—that's what Mrs. Simpson said."

"I'm not a hero," John Henry protested.

"You certainly are!" his mother said. "We'll be attending a luncheon meeting of the club."

"But I don't want to," John Henry argued.

"Of course you do!" his mother told him. "It's quite an honor."

At the meeting that afternoon, John Henry felt

embarrassed sitting at the head table. Members of the Pet Lovers Club kept smiling at him and acting as if he were someone special.

"We were hoping that Mrs. Pettigrew could be here for the presentation," Mrs. Simpson said to John Henry and his mother, "but I understand she'll be away for a few more days."

"Yes, ma'am," John Henry replied. Thank goodness for that, he thought.

"However, Mrs. Pettigrew's niece, Agnes Reynolds, will be here any minute to represent her," Mrs. Simpson continued. "We're so proud of you, John Henry."

John Henry nodded, but inside he felt horrible. Getting an award for rescuing a cat he had let out of the house! It just didn't seem right. Of course, he hadn't let Mouser out on purpose. He hadn't even seen her escape, in fact. It must have been when he was putting fresh water in her bowl.

"Oh, here comes Agnes now," Mrs. Simpson exclaimed, clinking her cup with her fork to get everyone's attention. "Ladies and gentlemen, it's time to make the presentation to our special guest!"

John Henry swallowed and looked around. Mrs. Simpson was smiling at him; Ms. Reynolds was smiling at him; everyone was smiling at him, acting as if he were a hero. John Henry couldn't stand it another second.

"I don't deserve to get an award," John Henry blurted out.

There was stunned silence in the hall.

"Mrs. Pettigrew asked me to feed Mouser while she was gone and not to let her out of the house," he went on, near tears.

"Well, I don't know how she got out, but she did and it was my fault, so I don't deserve to get an award." John Henry sat down next to his mother and stared at the plate.

"My goodness, is that what you think happened?" Ms. Reynolds asked. "You think *you* let Mouser out of the house?"

John Henry nodded.

"It wasn't you! My aunt called and asked me to go over and water her plants," Ms. Reynolds explained. "As I was going into the house, Mouser ran out. I tried to catch her, but she ran up that tree. I thought you knew!"

John Henry swallowed. "I didn't."

"So you're a hero after all!" Mrs. Simpson decided. "Come get your award, John Henry Colton."

Everyone clapped, and John Henry smiled happily. Hero or not, at least he hadn't broken his promise.

Alison Wants a Roommate

By Linda Way

Alison wanted a roommate, someone to share sunny days and rainstorms with. She took a board and painted the bright orange words ALISON WANTS A ROOMMATE. She nailed the sign to her picket fence. "That's an eye-catcher," she said. "Someone special will stop."

Alison was eating breakfast when she heard a

knock at the door. It was a goat. "What a tasty-looking house," he said. "First I'll eat your table, then your bed. That armchair will be my midnight snack."

"If you munch up all of my furniture, where will I sit and where will I sleep?" asked Alison.

"And what will I eat?" asked Goat.

"I don't want you for a roommate," Alison told Goat. "But I'll give you something sweet to munch on." Goat walked away nibbling Alison's old straw hat.

Alison took her bright orange paints, and to the sign that read ALISON WANTS A ROOMMATE she added NO EATING FURNITURE.

Soon Alison heard a loud roar. She opened the door just a bit, and there stood a lion with a shining mane.

"I'm looking for a home, and I don't eat furniture," he growled. Alison led him into the living room, where he gave such a loud roar that the house shook.

"You're too loud to be my roommate," Alison told him bravely.

"Loud!" roared Lion. "I'll show you loud!" He roared as loud as he could.

"STOP that! SCAT!" shouted Alison, and she shooed Lion out the door.

"Whew," gasped Alison when she was alone.

"Looking for a roommate can be hard work."

She took her orange paints, and to the sign that read ALISON WANTS A ROOMMATE, NO EATING FURNITURE she added NO ROARING.

It wasn't long before Alison heard some thumping on her welcome mat. It was a kangaroo with a baby in her pouch.

"We don't eat furniture, and we don't roar. All we do is hop, hop, hop," Mama Kangaroo said. She took a long tape measure from her pouch. "Your living room is two hops by three hops. Your kitchen is one hop by one hop. Baby and I need lots of jumping room. Your house is just too small," she said with a sad smile.

"Good-bye," called Alison. "I hope you find a good home." Alison took her orange paints, and to the sign that read ALISON WANTS A ROOMMATE, NO EATING FURNITURE, NO ROARING she added NO HOPPING.

Alison was playing the tuba when a hippo came to her door.

"How do you do?" he asked. He mopped his brow with a red bandanna. "I think I may be starving," he told her. "I haven't had a bite since tea, and that was an hour ago." Hippo sat down on the couch and three chairs, with his feet resting on a table. Alison made him a snack of twenty-seven watercress sandwiches and a dozen batches of brownies.

Hippo was taking his last bite of brownie when the milkman came. "Please leave twenty bottles of milk!" Hippo called out. "And all the bread you've got."

"Hippo," Alison told him firmly, "you need to find a home in a restaurant or a supermarket where there is plenty of food."

"Well, we had fun," Hippo reminded her. "Just give me your recipe for fudge brownies, and I'll be going." Hippo could barely get out the door.

Alison took her paints, and to the sign that read ALISON WANTS A ROOMMATE, NO EATING FURNITURE, NO ROARING, NO HOPPING she added NO OVEREATING.

What an exciting day! But Alison still didn't have a roommate. She snuggled under her quilt with her teddy bear. A light tap woke her from her dreams. There, in the cold, stood a fuzzy tiger kitten holding a suitcase.

"Hi," she said, "my name is Hildegarde. I need a home. I don't roar. I purr. I don't eat much, just a little milk. I don't hop. I leap lightly." With that she jumped into Alison's arms. "But what exactly is a roommate?" she asked Alison.

"A roommate," Alison told her, "is someone to share games on sunny days, rainstorms, and cocoa in bed with. If there are night noises, roommates check the cellar together holding hands."

"That's me!" Hildegarde shouted. "I'm all of that." And the two of them clapped and danced around the room. Hildegarde sang songs about gypsy cats from far away. They ate sardines and drank cocoa with marshmallows.

The next morning Alison woke up and got out her toolbox. She took down the sign that read ALISON WANTS A ROOMMATE, NO EATING FURNITURE, NO ROARING, NO HOPPING, NO OVEREATING.

She painted on the mailbox with her bright orange paints HILDEGARDE LIVES HERE!

Pilgrim Dog*

By Marcella Fisher Anderson

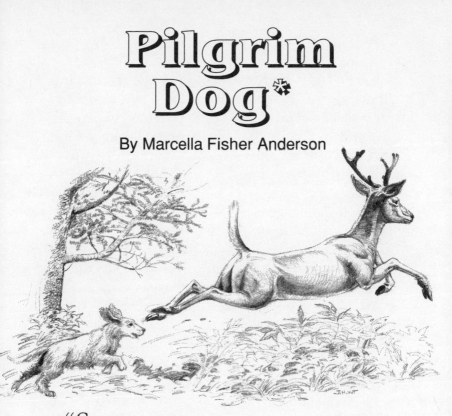

"So," said Father, standing with William on the deck of the *Mayflower* while the sails smacked in the wind above them, "I hear you have agreed to take care of John Goodman's spaniel when we reach America."

William looked up at him. "John says he'll have more important things to do than watch out for a dog that doesn't even have a name. He won't be trouble. He's just a dog."

"See to it then," said Father. "He will be your responsibility."

Sixty-five nights and days after leaving England, the lookout in the crow's-nest sighted land at last. The spaniel went ashore with John Goodman, Father, and some others looking for a place for the Pilgrims to settle.

When they got back to the ship, Father's lips were white with anger. "That dog frightened some Indians we saw. We wanted to let them know we are friendly. But that spaniel chased after their dog and scared them into the forest. That dog should never go ashore with us again. He should be named 'Indian-chaser.'"

"He's just a dog," said William.

By December the Pilgrims had found a good place to settle. One day in winter when the building had slowed because so many of the Pilgrims lay sick, John Goodman came for his dog to go along with him and Peter Browne while they collected rushes for roof thatching. Not until morning did the young men return.

"This dog," said Father, "chased a deer into the forest; and, chasing after *him,* the young men became lost. Never again should that dog go into the forest. He should be named 'Deerhunter.'"

"He's just a dog," said William.

When spring came, the Pilgrims planted corn

as their Indian friend Squanto had taught them. They planted the seed kernels in little hills, carefully covering each one with three small fish to fertilize the earth.

Very early one morning, the spaniel sniffed his way to the cornfield. He dug up the fish and all the newly planted corn.

This time Father shouted at William and the dog. "From now on, until the corn is as high as my waist, the dog is tied day and night, night and day. He should be called 'Corn-digger.'"

"He's just a dog," said William, feeling his heart heavy in his chest.

By August, the corn was high, the pumpkins were rounding out, and wild berries were ripening. It was nearly time for harvest. Governor Bradford called a meeting of all the Pilgrims. "We shall invite our Indian friend Massasoit and his men to share a harvest festival with us. The Indians will know then for certain that we are grateful for their help."

When the day of the great celebration arrived, Massasoit and ninety of his braves came out of the forest. William counted them.

The spaniel's fur bristled along his back, and a low growl started deep in his throat. Just as the dog gathered his hind legs to spring forward at a wolflike Indian dog, William's father kicked his foot in the spaniel's direction, sending the dog under one of the tables.

"And there he stays," commanded Father.

Very early on the third day of the celebration, William came out of his house; the dog stood up and followed him. Some of the Indians still lay sleeping about the fires, but a few were mixing cornmeal for their breakfast.

Just then, the spaniel darted forward. He ran past the Indian fires to the edge of the forest, where William could barely see a thin trail of smoke rising.

The dog put his nose to the ground and started sniffing. Disappearing into the trees, he dashed out again, carrying a burning stick in his mouth. He dropped the stick in the clearing, where one of the Indians shouted and stamped out the flames. Others ran into the forest to put out the blaze.

William's father came up beside him. "A spark from the fires set some leaves aflame. We might have lost the settlement."

William looked up at his father for praise for the spaniel, but Father said nothing.

When the Indians left at last, William was tired—tired of playing games, tired of keeping the fires going, tired even of eating. He closed the house door without so much as a glance at the dog and went to bed.

Much later, William awoke.

Father was calling out the door: "Just-a-Dog, Just-a-Dog!" Then he disappeared into the darkness. A moment later, he returned carrying the spaniel and sat down with him in front of the fire.

With pounding heart, William left the warmth of his blankets spread on the floor, and, shaking a little, huddled on the stool next to Father. William was worried that the dog had caused more trouble.

"You did well today, Just-a-Dog," Father said gently, lifting his hand to pat the dog's head.

The spaniel lifted his head and licked Father's hand.

"Who named you Just-a-Dog?" asked Father.

"You did, Father—just now," said William.

"Did I?" Father laughed. "I thought you called him that. From now on, Just-a-Dog, you may sleep indoors in front of the fire on cold nights like this one."

William had such a wide smile on his face that he could scarcely form the words to talk. "Rub him under the ears, Father," said William at last. "Just-a-Dog likes that best."

* The Pilgrims brought two dogs with them—a spaniel and a mastiff. The spaniel's first three exploits are described from writings in Pilgrim diaries.

The Fixit Team

By Linda Connor

Andrea Jones lived in the town of Big Sandy on the banks of the Swift River at the foot of Green Mountain. She looked like any other ten-year-old girl, but she wasn't. For one thing, Andrea enjoyed fixing things more than she enjoyed playing games. Furthermore, she was the only girl at Big Sandy Elementary School who owned an elephant. Not a stuffed elephant, mind you, but a real, live, peanut-eating, big-as-a-dump-truck elephant! His name was Cabot Arminius Ballyntyne.

Every day Andrea would rush home from school and up to her room. Then she would grab her toolbox, slide down the banister, dash through the kitchen, and run to the backyard, where Cabot would be waiting to go through their usual routine. First, Andrea would place the toolbox in front of Cabot, open it, and take out her checklist.

"Hammer, nails, screwdriver, saw," she would call out, and Cabot would find each tool and check to see that it was ready to use.

As soon as the last item was called, Andrea would say, "Okay, Cabot, out with the advertising!" and Cabot would bring the blanket Andrea had made for him from his stall. It was bright red, with letters that read

Andrea and Cabot would arrange the blanket on Cabot's back, then Cabot would lift Andrea onto the blanket. Finally, when the toolbox was hanging from Cabot's trunk, Andrea would shout, "Move 'em out!" and off they would go, up and down the streets of Big Sandy.

When they first started these job hunts, Andrea and Cabot didn't get any work. People were kind and always shouted "Hello," but when something broke, they would call other repair services to do the work. Andrea and Cabot would return home for supper without having done a single job for a single person.

If Andrea had been an ordinary person, she would have been very discouraged. She probably would have stayed home and taken up skateboarding. But Andrea was not an ordinary person.

"Chin up, Cabot," she would say. "Those grown-ups just aren't used to us yet. We know we can fix things, and someday we will get our chance."

Sure enough, one day as they were going up Fifteenth Street, Mrs. Hinklemeyer ran out to the curb and cried out, "Oh, I am so glad you came by today, Andrea dear! My cat is stuck in the maple tree, and the fire department is too busy to come right away with their big ladder. I am much too worried about my poor dear Precious to leave him there all afternoon! Do you think you could help me out?"

Andrea was excited, but she managed to say in her most businesslike voice, "Be glad to, Mrs. Hinklemeyer. Now, if you will just lead us to the tree, please, Cabot and I will do our best to resolve your difficulties. Move 'em out, Cabot!"

When they got to the maple tree, it was a simple matter for Andrea to stand on Cabot's head, reach into the tree, and pluck Precious from his perch. Then Cabot gently put Andrea and Precious on the ground right in front of Mrs. Hinklemeyer. The poor woman was so grateful that she had tears in her eyes. She paid Andrea and even gave her a fifty-cent tip!

Andrea was so elated over the Fixit Team's first job that she decided to go home the long way and stop at O'Brien's Grocery Store for ice-cream cones. "We'll treat ourselves to celebrate," she said to Cabot as they turned the corner onto Main Street.

"Help!" she heard someone call. It was Mr. O'Brien himself, standing on tiptoe outside his grocery store, trying to keep the big swinging sign from falling down. The wind had blown one end right off its hook and the sign had almost knocked Arthur Billings's mother off the sidewalk. It *had* knocked a big bag of groceries out of her arms and all over the street.

"Help me, Andrea!" Mr. O'Brien shouted.

"Nothing to it," Andrea answered. "We'll take care of it right away."

First Cabot opened the toolbox and removed some wire. He handed it up to Andrea. Then he held the sign while she replaced it on the hook and wired it securely in place.

Mr. O'Brien helped Mrs. Billings with her groceries while the Fixit Team worked. When they were finished, he said, "Great job, Andrea. Thank you, Cabot." And, on top of their usual fee, he gave them each a gooseberry ice-cream cone for a tip. "I'll keep you two in mind the next time I need help."

That night Andrea went to bed still glowing with pride over the Fixit Team's first jobs. She dreamed all night about the jobs she and Cabot would get in the future, and about gooseberry ice-cream-cone tips.

look, he discovered that Daisy's calf was being born. Even worse, it was being born backward.

Mark had seen Dad help a cow deliver a breech calf last spring, and he knew that the calf could drown in birth fluids before its head was born. He knelt in the grass behind Daisy and grasped the legs of the calf, just as Dad had done. Daisy lifted her head and gazed back at him helplessly. A difficult birth could mean death for her and her calf.

Mark's stomach was churning. He dug his heels into the sod and pulled hard. Daisy pushed. A few inches of the calf slid out. He felt as if he were trying to pull a hundred-pound sack of feed through a knothole.

He remembered that it was important to work fast on a breech delivery. Mark threw himself backward, tugging on the calf's legs. A few more inches of its chest appeared. Sweat burned in Mark's eyes, and his arms ached.

This is taking too long, Mark thought. Maybe I can't do it.

Daisy pushed again, and Mark pulled with every ounce of his strength.

A moment later a beautiful black-and-white heifer calf flopped onto the grass. She would grow into a great milking cow like her mom, Mark thought. And he had saved her by himself.

He sat in the grass wriggling the stiffness out

of his fingers. The calf lay still, eyes wide and glassy. Mark looked closer. Something was wrong.

"Oh no!" Mark gasped. "She isn't breathing." He felt the slow thump-thump of her heart when he held his hand on her chest.

He grabbed a weed stem and frantically inserted it into the calf's nose to make the animal sneeze and start breathing. No response. He tried lifting her up by her back legs to drain the fluid from her lungs. Dead weight. Mark couldn't get even half of the hundred-pound calf off the ground.

"I saved your life!" Mark screamed. "Now breathe!" He pounded on the calf's chest, knowing in a minute she might be dead.

"Mark, what's wrong?" Dad shouted from the driveway. He ran toward the field.

"Daisy's calf won't breathe. She's dying!" Hot tears stung Mark's eyes. Seconds dragged between the heartbeats. The calf was drowning from the birth fluid in its lungs. How can I lose her now? Mark thought.

Suddenly he remembered his swimming instructor's words. "Give mouth-to-mouth resuscitation," the instructor always said. "Ask questions later." If it worked with swimmers, it just might work with breech calves.

Mark shuddered at the thought of putting his

mouth on the calf's slimy wet nose. But he held her face between his hands, one palm covering a nostril. With his eyes squeezed shut, he blew into the other nostril. Again. And again.

The calf sputtered, sneezed . . . and took a breath.

"Way to go!" Dad cried as he reached them. "You saved that calf's life. I never would have thought of trying that."

"It worked. It's a heifer," Mark said. He wiped his mouth on his shirt, trying not to think about that big wet nose he had just kissed. His heart felt three times too big for his chest. He had saved a life.

"She's your calf," Dad said, helping Mark to his feet. "We'll register her in your name. What will you call her?"

Mark watched Daisy nuzzle and lick her new calf. He gazed toward the farm he loved, with its huge barn full of work, and grinned at Dad.

"I'll name her Breathless," Mark said. "She's going to be the best cow on our farm."

Dolphin Emergency

By Susan March

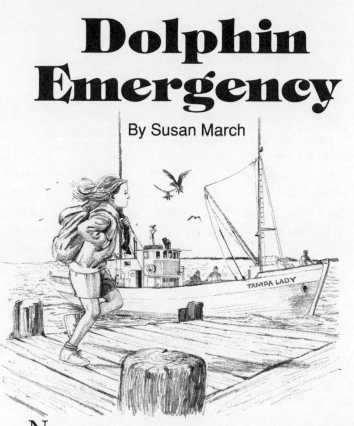

Nickie Ortega swung the bag of skipjack fish over her shoulder and headed for the door.

"Thanks, Mr. Beta," she called. "The dolphins will love them. Yesterday's fish snack was sea robins, but they didn't eat them. They like the skipjack, though."

Nickie started down the street toward the

docks. It was late afternoon, and the sponge fishermen would be coming in soon. It was the off-season, and most of the Tarpon Springs tourists had left for home. The waterfront would be nearly deserted until the hustle of docking sponge boats began. Nickie wanted to be there in time to greet her father, with a few minutes extra for feeding her dolphin friends.

Rounding the corner, Nickie came in sight of the docks. "One of the boats is back already!" she said aloud. Drawing closer, she read the name *Tampa Lady*. The fishermen had pulled their nets down and off the boat. "It's a fishing boat," Nickie said with surprise. She knew little about fishing boats, but she could see that the nets were badly torn and tangled.

"Hey!" she called. "What happened?"

"Dolphins!" one of the men grumbled. "We had a good catch out past the wreck and were ready to haul in when three hungry dolphins drove into the school. When we pulled in the nets, they tore holes in them. We lost everything."

"That's right," another said. "Tomorrow we go out with guns. We'll teach them not to steal our fish and ruin our nets."

Nickie turned away in silence. She knew the playful pranks of the dolphins, but fishermen seldom came into the sponging waters. It had been a long time since there had been complaints of dolphin trouble. The sponge divers welcomed dolphins as Neptune's friends and protectors against sharks. Stories were told of dolphins warning ships of approaching storms and rescuing drowning sailors.

Nickie stared out at the water. The familiar fins and flapping tails were nowhere in sight. They must have been scared off by the fishermen, she thought. But tomorrow they will have forgotten their danger. Tomorrow they will be hunted and shot.

Tears welled in Nickie's eyes. She thought of going back to the fishermen, of begging them not to shoot the dolphins. But it would be useless. They could not understand. They would only think of their lost fish and torn nets. A young girl's sentiment would mean little.

Nickie started back toward town. She couldn't greet her father with tears. She must think of a way to save the dolphins.

Tomorrow is Saturday, she thought. The dolphins will be in the cove. If I can keep them there until the fishermen have given up their hunt, they will be safe until Monday. Mario will help me, she said to herself.

Mario owned the fish market in Tarpon Springs. He often joined Nickie when she went to feed the dolphins. He would understand. He would think of some way to protect the dolphins.

Nickie slammed the fish market door. "Mario, Mario!" she called. Mario's wife, Nina, came out of the back room.

"Mario went to Marco Island this morning," she said. "He won't be back until tomorrow."

"When tomorrow?" Nickie moaned.

"Early. Very early. Around four o'clock in the morning," Nina answered.

"I'll be here to meet him," Nickie said. "I'm late for supper, but tell him there's a dolphin emergency and I need his help. I'll tell him more when I see him."

Nina nodded, and Nickie hurried toward home.

It was still dark when Nickie's alarm clock rang at 3:30. She had slept in her clothes so she could start for Mario's without wasting time dressing.

Mario will know what to do, Nickie told herself. But her heart pounded with the secret fear that what she was doing was hopeless.

Nickie ran over to Mario's truck when she saw the bright headlights pull up to the curb.

"Nina called and told me there was a dolphin emergency," Mario said.

"Yes," Nickie answered. "Some Tampa fishermen are mad at the dolphins because they stole their fish and ruined the nets. They're going to shoot them. If we can keep the dolphins in the cove today, they will be safe. But I don't know how we can do it."

"I do," Mario answered. "There's no time to waste, though. You start for the cove. I'll meet you there after I get some things together."

Nickie was wading in the water and calling to the dolphins when Mario's old truck pulled into sight. It was loaded down with fish, inner tubes, and other junk from the dump.

"With these we can keep the dolphins' interest so they'll stay in the cove," Mario explained. "I've sometimes spent hours watching them push

51

inner tubes around in the water."

It was six o'clock and time for supper when Nickie headed for home. Mario's idea had worked. The dolphins were safe until Monday. But what would save them then? Nickie would be in school. Mario would have to work. There would be no one to keep the dolphins in the cove.

Nickie neared the docks. There was the fishing boat—the *Tampa Lady!*

"Didn't see any dolphins today," the men were saying. "But those sharks were worse. Scared off all the fish. We didn't catch a thing. The fishing is really bad around here."

Nickie felt her heart pound. Maybe the *Tampa Lady* would fish somewhere else.

"We'll give it a try for the next couple of days at least," the captain said. "There are fish out there."

"I didn't see the dolphins either," one of the sponge divers said. "Could be that's why you had so much shark trouble. We saw two big ones coming in from the Gulf. Dolphins sometimes keep sharks away by ramming them—saved my life more than once that way."

"But they ruin our nets," the fishermen said.

"Not if you're careful. The dolphin herds can usually be seen from a distance, and you can get your nets in before they do damage. It's not so easy, but it's better than chancing torn nets, bad catches, and sharks."

"Yes, that sounds okay," the skipper said.

Nickie smiled. The dolphins would be safe. The fishermen would understand now about her dolphins.

A Regular Railroad Dog

By Avis J. Kirsch

Trigger was a railroad dog right from the start. Charlie, the station agent, found the black-and-white cocker spaniel in a deserted boxcar.

Before he adopted Trigger, Charlie was frequently lonesome. He worked at a small railroad station high up in the Rocky Mountains of Colorado. He was the flagman, switchman, and yardmaster. He was everything, because there was no one else.

One of Charlie's duties was to turn the switch, and Trigger went with him. It was an important task. At the switch the trains could go on the right track fork to the gold fields or on the left track fork to the silver mines. Charlie knew which way to turn the switch by the number of toots signaled to him by the engineer.

Hearing those engine whistles all the time, Trigger learned to tell them apart. Whenever they sounded, he ran to the switch. With his little head cocked to one side and his black-and-white tail straight up, he'd watch Charlie open the correct switch.

Trigger took such an interest in the switching that Charlie made a decision. "I'm going to teach you how to lift the handle with your nose and move it with your paws."

Before long, Trigger could do it alone.

Charlie discovered a section of track that needed repair. When the men came out to work on the rails, Charlie showed them how Trigger could turn the switch.

They took off their caps and scratched their heads. It was hard for them to believe what they were seeing.

"Charlie, you got yourself a regular railroad dog," one of the men said.

While the men were working, Charlie had to stop the train, so he'd stand in the middle of the tracks and wave a red flag.

Trigger went with Charlie each time and stood beside him. Soon Charlie let Trigger carry the flag. Then the dog learned to fetch it. By the time the repairs were almost finished, Trigger would get the flag, sit up between the rails holding the flag in his teeth, and wait for the big iron locomotive to stop. Sometimes the big monster of an engine, bellowing steam, would come very close to the little dog before it stopped, but Trigger never faltered. He'd hold still until the iron wheels came to a screeching halt. Then he'd wag his tail and go back to the station.

"A regular railroad dog," the men said, over and over.

One bitter-cold winter day when the wind blew with an icy breath, Charlie's knees began to hurt. When he heard the train coming up the mountain, he started out for the switch. It was very painful for Charlie to walk.

Trigger scampered along, his curly black ears flopping in the biting wind. But when they reached the switch, Trigger could not move it.

"What's the matter, Trigger?" Charlie asked.

Then he saw. The switch was frozen in the middle. The train coming could not go on the left or the right fork. It would wreck. Charlie tugged with all his might, but the switch did not move.

"Old 49 will be here before I can get the red flag," Charlie said.

The engineer was signaling for the left fork. Expecting to go to the silver mines, he would instead shoot straight ahead and down the mountain.

"Trigger, Mr. Sears, the superintendent of the railroad, is on Old 49. And all the others will go down, too! Quick, Trigger, fetch the flag!"

The little dog started running back to the station.

"Hurry!" shouted Charlie above the howling wind.

Trigger ran faster.

In spite of the weather, little beads of sweat formed on Charlie's forehead. He had never been so scared. Could Trigger save the train? He closed his eyes and said a prayer. The sound of the train pounding on the rails thundered in Charlie's head.

Tugging its load of passengers, the engine labored upward. "Now it's at the bend," Charlie said aloud. "It'll come roaring by me on the downgrade and hit that spot where the track divides, and over they'll go—people, boxcars, engine, strewn all over the mountainside."

Charlie hated to open his eyes, but when he did . . . there was Trigger in the center of the track, sitting proudly on his hind legs, his two little paws showing like white mittens, the red flag secure in his mouth.

Closer and closer the engine came, its great iron point aimed like an arrow at the brave little dog. Sparks flew from the wheels as the engineer tried to apply the brakes.

Inches from Trigger, the train stopped.

Charlie was a man who never let his feelings show, but this time they overwhelmed him. He hobbled over to Trigger, picked up the little dog, flag and all, and hugged him. "You did it, Trigger. You did it!"

Mr. Sears hopped off the train, wanting to know why it had stopped. When he heard about Trigger, Mr. Sears petted the dog and said, "This wee laddie saved all our lives. I'm going to send him a big, juicy steak every day for as long as he lives."

Some say this is a true story. They say it happened at Forks Creek, Colorado, in 1900, and the real Trigger stopped that train. "A regular railroad dog," they say.

How One Rabbit Got Its Name

By Lenna Cloud Mueller

Smiling, Miss Wilson faced her class. "Your assignment is to write a letter to Mr. Moody, thanking him for giving us the rabbit for a pet," she said. "Tell Mr. Moody what you would like to call the rabbit.

"I will take all the letters to his home after school. He has agreed to choose the three most interesting names tonight and call me. Tomorrow we will vote for the name we like best."

Thinking hard about what she would write, Doris reached for her pencil. Although she'd been at Cedar Ridge School for a month, she was still called "the new girl." She wished they would call her Doris.

Doris, whose parents were from China, had lived in San Francisco, where there were many others from the big Yee family. Then her family had moved to Missouri. Doris liked Missouri, but it was different from California. There were no Yees in Missouri except Doris and her mother and father. In Missouri she couldn't see the Pacific Ocean, run on the beach, or feed bread crumbs to the screeching sea gulls. She missed seeing the Golden Gate Bridge and Chinatown. But most of all she missed her big family and friends.

Her mother had told her to be patient. "Friends are not made in a day," she had said. But many days had passed, and Doris still felt out of place.

Doris was so busy writing her letter that Miss Wilson had to speak to her twice. "Have you finished your letter, Doris?" she asked.

"Yes, Miss Wilson," Doris replied. It was a good letter, she thought. It was neat and polite, and she hadn't forgotten the date.

Miss Wilson asked the class to read their letters aloud and then write the names they had chosen on the chalkboard.

Dianne was first. She wrote *Rudolph Rabbit.*

Robert was next. He wrote *Mickey.* Ralph wrote *Hopalong.*

David wrote *Speedy.*

"You're next, Doris," Miss Wilson said.

Doris got to her feet and proudly read her letter, beginning with the date, Year of the Dragon 4674.

There was a moment of stunned silence, followed by a roar of laughter. Doris's heart sank.

Miss Wilson rapped on the desk. "Quiet," she said sternly. "Doris has brought to our attention something we should know. We use the Gregorian calendar, but there are others, such as the Hebrew, Islamic, and Chinese calendars. According to the Chinese calendar, it is the Year of the Dragon 4674. Thank you, Doris, for reminding us of this interesting fact."

The classroom was unusually quiet as Doris continued to read:

Dear Mr. Moody:

Thank you for giving us the rabbit. You are very kind and very wise. I would like to call our rabbit Old Mr. Moody.

Again, there was stunned silence, followed by a roar of laughter.

David got to his feet. "I don't think we should send that letter to Mr. Moody," he said. "It sounds rude to me. I think Mr. Moody would be insulted to have our rabbit called Old Mr. Moody."

Doris's face felt hot, her mouth went dry, and a big lump filled her throat.

"My letter is not rude," she defended herself. "I was paying a compliment to Mr. Moody."

"Some compliment!" David retorted.

"Doris's letter is excellent," Miss Wilson said. "Of course we shall send it."

Doris trudged to the chalkboard and wrote *Old Mr. Moody*. With her head lowered, she returned to her desk and sat quietly while the rest of the letters and names were read.

At home that night Doris told her father about the letter. "They laughed at me, and I was embarrassed," she said.

"Perhaps you should have explained why you chose the name," her father said.

Doris tried to do her homework, but she kept thinking about the letter. More than anything, she wanted David to be her friend, but David thought she was rude.

Suddenly she remembered what her father had said. That was the answer.

At school the next morning, Miss Wilson said, "Mr. Moody has selected the three most interesting names for our rabbit. I have written them on the chalkboard."

Looking at the chalkboard, Doris saw *Rudolph Rabbit* and *Hopalong* and—she couldn't believe her eyes—*Old Mr. Moody*.

"Before we vote," Miss Wilson said, "I want Dianne, Ralph, and Doris to tell us why they selected their particular names."

"I chose Rudolph Rabbit because it sounds nice," said Dianne.

"Hopalong describes how a rabbit moves," Ralph said. "Everyone has seen our rabbit hop."

It was Doris's turn. She realized that Miss Wilson had given her the opportunity she needed to explain. She concentrated, trying to remember the right words.

"For many years my father has told me that the Chinese people have many good customs. They are different from American customs. Sometimes it is not easy to understand them. In China it is a great honor to be called old. It is an honor because when people grow old in years, they also grow in kindness and wisdom.

"Mr. Moody is kind because he gave us the rabbit. He is wise because he has lived many years and has learned many lessons that we have not yet learned. When I named our rabbit Old Mr. Moody, I tried to say Mr. Moody is kind and wise. He should be loved and revered."

Doris sat down. The classroom was very still.

David raised his hand. "I want to apologize for saying Doris's letter was rude," he said. "I am sorry I did not understand. I think Old Mr. Moody is a fine name. I'm going to vote for it."

"I am, too," Dianne said.

"So am I," said Ralph.

Everyone was looking at Doris and smiling. She was so happy she thought she would burst.

"I wish we could change the Chinese

66

calendar," Robert said. "The year 4674 should be the Year of the Rabbit."

Everyone laughed.

"Shall we vote now?" asked Miss Wilson.

It was unanimous for Doris and Old Mr. Moody.

The Queen
of 104

By Marilyn Bissell

The alarm clock rang, and Ricky got out of bed. He could smell toast and bacon. He put on his robe and went downstairs.

"Morning, Mom," Ricky said, rubbing his eyes.

"You can go back to bed if you want," said his mother. "We had a storm last night and there's no school today."

"No!" Ricky said.

"No?" said his mother. "I thought you'd be happy."

"But, Mom," said Ricky, "Regina might have her babies today!"

"Who's Regina?" asked Mom.

"She's the mother guppy in our aquarium. Mrs. Davis says *Regina* means 'queen' in Latin," explained Ricky. "Regina's the queen of our room at school."

"But what's this about babies?"

"Regina is going to have baby guppies soon— maybe today. If we don't get them out of the aquarium right away, Regina will *eat* them! That's what guppies do."

"How terrible," said Mom. "But I'm afraid there's nothing you can do. School is closed. Some neighborhoods don't even have power for heat or light."

"Oh no!" exclaimed Ricky. "If the water in the aquarium gets too cold, Regina could freeze."

The doorbell rang. It was Tom, Ricky's friend. Tom stamped snow off his boots and came in.

"Are you going out to play?"

"We can't play, Tom. We have to save Regina."

"Save her from what?" asked Tom.

"Wait here while I get dressed. We have to go to school and get her or Regina might freeze."

Ricky was dressed in no time and quickly

pulled on his boots and winter jacket.

"We're going over to school, Mom," called Ricky.

"But no one will be there," said Mom.

"Maybe somebody will. We'll be back soon."

The boys had a hard time walking the three blocks to school. The wind had piled the snow high in some places, and it was starting to snow again.

The school was dark and there were no cars in the teachers' lot.

"There's nobody here," Tom said.

"Let's see if the door is open."

They trudged around to the front door and tried it. It was locked.

"What do we do now?" asked Tom.

"Let's try to look in the window," replied Ricky.

Room 104 was on the first floor on the east side of the school. The boys followed their footprints back around the school until they came to the windows of their room.

"It's too high," said Tom.

"Give me a boost," said Ricky. "If I can just hold on to the sill for a minute, I'll be able to see Regina."

Tom made a little shelf out of his hands and Ricky stepped on it and reached up for the sill. It took three tries, but at last he got a good hold and looked inside. There was Regina swimming around in the water. The light on the aquarium was off!

Ricky dropped down into the snow, knocking Tom over.

"If the tank light is off, then the heat is off, too, and Regina will get cold soon," said Ricky. "Let's go home and think of a plan."

Ricky's mother had cocoa ready for the boys. They sat in the kitchen and tried to think of a way to help Regina.

"Mrs. Davis!" shouted Ricky. "We'll call Mrs. Davis!"

"I'm afraid you can't," Mom said. "She lives south of the city, and the phone lines are down in that area. It will take a long time to fix."

"Oh!" said Ricky, pounding his fist on the table. "There must be *somebody* who could open the door for us."

Suddenly, Tom started to smile. "I've got it," he said. "We can call Smiley."

"Do you mean the janitor?" asked Mom.

"Sure."

"Well, let's find his number in the phone book. I'm sure he'll help you."

Ricky got the big phone book out and started to turn pages. "Uh-oh," he said.

"What's the matter?"

"Do you know Smiley's last name?"

"Hmm," said Tom, thinking hard. "I think it starts with a D, and it reminds me of cars. Think of words about cars. Let's see, tire-Dire, wheel-

73

Deal, hub-Dub. . ."

Ricky tried. "Jack-Dack, brake-Drake. Oh, Tom, are you sure it starts with a D?"

"Positive. Let's see. Lock-Dock, key-Dee. . . ."

"I can't think of any more, Tom. Cars just remind me of gas and oil."

"That's it!" exclaimed Tom. "Oil-Doyle. Smiley Doyle!"

"Phew! Am I glad," said Ricky, finding the page with Doyle on it—*lots* of Doyles.

"Oh, boy," he said. "You don't know his real first name, do you?"

"No," replied Tom. "But I know he lives over the store on Elm Street."

Ricky ran his finger down the page until he came to *Doyle Michael 237 Elm - - - - 555-2818*.

Fortunately, Smiley was at home. Ricky told him all about Regina, and before the boys had their outdoor clothes on, Smiley was there in his Jeep to pick them up. He found the right key on the huge ring, and they were soon inside Room 104. Regina was swimming slowly, and the room was cold.

They emptied most of the water from the aquarium so that the glass wouldn't crack when they moved it. Smiley drove slowly back to Ricky's house, trying not to slosh Regina around too much.

The boys carried the aquarium into the house

and put it on the kitchen counter. Soon Regina would be safe and warm!

Smiley and the boys ate cookies and watched Regina swim around and around in the aquarium.

Suddenly, tiny dots appeared in the water.

"The babies!" cried Ricky. He hurried to get the small fishbowl and net they'd brought from school. Smiley and Tom looked on as Ricky fished the baby guppies out of the tank and put them into the bowl. The three of them watched the tiny guppies swim.

"See the one that swims real fast?" asked Ricky, pointing.

Tom and Smiley nodded.

"I think we'll name him after Smiley—Prince Smiley of 104!"

Doggone Magic

By Judith Enderle

Amy looked down the street. There was no sign of her father. "I wish he'd hurry," said Amy.

She felt her shirt pocket. The small brown envelope was still there. She took it out. Across the bottom it said *You will find your magic surprise inside. Eat MUNCHY NUGGETS for a "magic" breakfast.*

Amy's friend Karen had a brown envelope, too. They were going to open them together. They had promised to wait and do it at the same time.

"What could the surprise be?" wondered Amy. She pinched the envelope. It was lightly padded, and she couldn't tell what was in it.

Amy looked down the street again. Mrs. Perkins, a neighbor, was coming from across the way. She seemed upset.

"Amy, have you seen Aristotle? I can't find him anywhere," she said.

"No, I haven't," said Amy, "but I'll watch for him on my way to Karen's house. I'll be leaving as soon as my dad gets back from the grocery store with my bike."

"A Great Dane simply cannot disappear," said Mrs. Perkins, shaking her head. She went down the street, looking beneath parked cars and behind bushes. "Aristotle! Aristotle!" she called.

Amy turned around in time to see her father ride into the drive. He almost collided with another neighbor, Mr. Ezra, whose worried frown made his eyebrows look like one fuzzy line across his forehead.

"Have you seen my Dusty?" he asked. Dusty was his Labrador retriever.

"I haven't seen her," said Amy's father.

"I know Dusty," said Amy, "but I haven't seen

her either. I'll watch for her on my way to Karen's house. I'm going there now."

Amy helped carry the groceries in. She was just leaving when the phone rang.

"It's for you, Amy."

Amy ran back inside.

"This is Karen. Hurry over."

"I can't hear you very well," Amy said. "There's too much noise at your house."

"Please hurry. I need you!" shouted Karen.

"I was just leaving!" Amy shouted back.

On the way Amy met the Haywood twins. "We've lost Itsy and Bitsy, our white poodles," they said. "Have you seen them?"

"You, too?" Amy said. "All the dogs in the neighborhood must be hiding this morning."

What Amy said seemed to be true. Before she reached Karen's house, she met Kim Soo, who was looking for Lady, and Mrs. Tessler, who was looking for Panda and Duffee.

Butch was missing from the Barton house, and Mrs. Jones said that Pixie had disappeared from her yard.

Amy turned the corner to Karen's house. She stopped and stared. The front yard, the front walk, and the front porch were full of dogs, including all the dogs that were missing from Amy's block.

"Help!" Karen called from behind the screen door.

"What are all these dogs doing here?" asked Amy. She dropped her bike at the edge of the lawn and squeezed through all the furry bodies.

Karen looked embarrassed. She held up a familiar brown envelope. "I couldn't stand the suspense. I didn't wait for you. I opened mine."

"What was in it?" asked Amy.

"This." Karen held up a thin silver whistle.

Amy took out her envelope and opened it. She had a whistle, too. She put it to her mouth.

"Stop! Don't blow it!" shouted Karen.

"Why not?" asked Amy.

"The whistle doesn't seem to make any noise. I thought mine was broken. I blew and blew. Then the dogs started coming. That's the magic. We can't hear it, but the dogs can. My brother says this kind of whistle makes a sound too high for humans to hear. But dogs can hear it just fine."

"Come on out," said Amy. "I'll help you return the dogs to their owners."

"You aren't angry because I didn't wait for you?"

"I was a little bit, but I'm not now. Can you imagine what would have happened if we'd both blown our magic whistles?"

"Stampede," said Karen. "These whistles have powerful magic. Dogs appear from everywhere."

"These whistles have doggone powerful magic," said Amy. "These are all missing mutts. Their owners are looking for them."

"*Dog-gone*? As in *missing mutts*?" Karen groaned. "That was a corny joke, Amy. Almost as funny as all these dogs."

The Uninvited Guests

By Michele Spence

Joey put the grass-catcher and power mower away and locked the shed. It was the end of two months of work on Mr. Reiger's yard. Down at Center Lake, chained to the dock, was Mr. Reiger's fishing boat with the three-horsepower motor. In return for his yard work, Joey would have the boat to use for a month.

He was finishing the edging as Mr. Reiger's van pulled up.

"Hi, Joey. Good job as usual, I see."

"Thanks, Mr. Reiger," Joey answered.

"Last day of the job. You've done fine work," Mr. Reiger said. "Whew, it's hot already, isn't it?"

Joey thought of the cool breeze that would be at the lake, the boat skimming across the water, and the weedy patch where he had seen the enormous largemouth bass leap.

"Here you are, Joey," Mr. Reiger said, pulling the key to the boat's padlock from his pocket.

"Boy, thanks."

"You deserve it. I don't know anyone who would have worked harder or longer than you have," Mr. Reiger remarked. "Have a good time. Be careful."

"I will. I will. I'll take good care of everything," Joey exclaimed. He jumped on his bike and pedaled down the highway toward Center Lake.

At the lake Joey saw that the boat was backed into the weeds. He grabbed the rope and began to pull it in. There was a sudden movement. Joey jumped back, thinking there might be a snake. No, too big, he decided. The movement was in the shade of a big live oak that hung over the water. It was a duck—crouched low, staring at him, and making a hissing sound.

The duck backed up and sat down. It was a mottled brown and tan, certainly not a farm bird.

It must be a wild one, Joey thought. He remembered his biology teacher saying that pintails lived in southern Georgia. But what was one doing down here?

The duck stood up. It walked to the edge of the boat. And there was the male, the drake, paddling around the stern. He was bigger than the female and a darker blackish brown. Around his neck was a bright flash of white collar, and on his wings green and lighter tan.

Joey looked back at the boat. What was it that the duck had been sitting on? It looked like Spanish moss. Joey squinted against the setting sun. In the nest there were eggs. They were a grayish green, exactly the color of the moss.

And then it hit him. The duck was in *his* boat. What was he going to do? Maybe he could move the nest to the weeds. Would that make the female abandon them? What a stupid thing to happen. Dumb duck, he thought. No telling how long it would be before they hatched. Well, there was nothing to do about it this evening. Hot disappointment rose in him. He suddenly felt very tired.

The next day after his biology class, Joey spoke to Mrs. Ross.

"Yes. That does sound like a pintail," said Mrs. Ross.

"Do you think there's any way to move the

nest out of the boat?" Joey asked.

"No way you can do that without putting the young in danger," the teacher replied.

Joey thought, I could move it anyway. The world could do without a few more ducks. That boat's mine. I worked for it. But even as he thought these things, he knew he would never do it. It just wouldn't be right.

After school, as Joey rode toward home, he passed the cutoff to Center Lake. "Might as well go see what those ducks are doing," he said.

The female saw him coming but seemed to be less nervous. The male still paddled nearby, searching in the weeds for food. Joey sat watching them till it was time to go home.

Each day after that Joey found himself back at the lake. Mrs. Ross said it would be about three weeks before the eggs would hatch. After the last day of school, Joey spent his time lying on his stomach on the dock in the sun. He often brought a picnic lunch and his fishing gear. Sometimes he walked down the shore and caught enough panfish to take home for dinner. But, of course, no bass, since he couldn't use the boat to get out to where they were.

Joey accepted the fact that he wasn't going to be able to use the boat and began to look forward to the birth of the ducklings. On the day it happened, the duck moved off her nest, and, where there had been a greenish egg, there was now a bright patch of wiggling yellow. Over the next hour, the other eggs were broken by the little beaks. Soon the mother helped the young over the edge of the boat and into the water. The ducklings formed a line behind the drake and her and were led away to feed.

Joey watched, fascinated. He had to sit on his hands to keep from applauding. He felt as proud as a new father himself.

"Those are pretty baby ducklings, Mama," he whispered softly.

Even though the boat still belonged to Joey for a while longer, he decided to leave it in case the ducks still needed the nest. He turned his bike toward home. At the unpaved road that led to his house, he stopped at the mailbox. In it was an envelope with his name on it, and inside was a single sheet of paper.

Dear Joey,

I wanted to let you know that we wouldn't be in town for a couple of weeks. We were called away for a conference on a new contract. Your teacher, Mrs. Ross, told me about the ducks in my boat. That was a fine thing you did, Joey. I know how much using the boat meant to you.

I won't have much time for fishing this summer, and I'm going to need more yard help. How about this, Joey? You come over for two hours every morning to help out, and you can use the boat anytime you want for the rest of the summer. You can watch those baby ducklings grow up while you're catching that big bass.

See you soon,

Bob Reiger

Joey let out a low whistle and grinned so wide

he didn't think he'd ever be able to stop.

"Well," he said aloud, "I guess sometimes you really can have things both ways." This was going to be a perfect summer.

A Dog for Belinda Bean

By Jean Davis

Ever since Belinda Bean could remember, she had wanted a dog. A big dog or a small dog. A spotted dog or a plain dog. A dog with long hair or short hair. Just any dog a girl would be proud to own.

But unfortunately for Belinda, her parents didn't feel the same way.

"A dog would dig up my flower beds and shed hair on the carpet," Mrs. Bean said. "And a dog might even bite Georgie!" Georgie was Belinda's three-year-old brother.

"A dog," said Mr. Bean, "would bark at night and keep everyone awake. And dogs cost money!"

Belinda begged for a dog so often that her parents finally said, "Not another word about dogs, Belinda!"

But Belinda couldn't help wishing.

One morning after breakfast, Belinda asked her mother if she could go to the pond near her house to fish.

"Yes, Belinda, but please be careful. That pond is deep."

"I'll be careful," Belinda promised. "And besides, I can swim."

"Me, too!" yelled Georgie. "Georgie go fish!"

"Oh, no!" laughed Mrs. Bean. "When you're as big as Belinda, then you can go to the pond to fish."

Georgie didn't like that one bit. He banged the table with his spoon and wouldn't finish his oatmeal.

"Bye, Mom," said Belinda, taking her fishing pole and starting for the door. But when she opened the door, she forgot all about fishing.

There on the steps was a dog!

And such a dog! His coat was covered with mud and burrs, and he was so skinny his ribs stuck out. He wagged his tail and looked hopefully at Belinda out of sad brown eyes.

"Look, Mom, look!" Belinda shouted. "There's a dog here!"

"What?" exclaimed Mrs. Bean, coming to see for herself. "Shoo him away, Belinda! He looks terrible!"

"He just needs a bath and some breakfast, Mom," Belinda said. "He doesn't have a collar, so he must be a stray. Please may I give him something to eat?"

Mrs. Bean looked into two pairs of pleading brown eyes. "All right. You may feed him. But when your father comes home for lunch, he'll have to take the dog to the animal shelter."

Belinda was glad she could keep the dog for a little while, anyway.

She filled a bowl with scraps from the breakfast table—a bit of toast with jam, the rest of Georgie's oatmeal, a strip of leftover bacon.

The dog gobbled the food down hungrily and then licked Belinda's face.

"Come on, dog," Belinda called. "You need a bath!"

They raced around to the front yard, where Belinda turned on the hose and scrubbed the dog all over.

"There!" said Belinda. "You look much better."

The dog did look better. His coat was shiny, his eyes sparkled, and he held his tail high. He looked like a dog any girl would be proud to own.

Now the dog was clean, but Belinda was not! Her shirt and jeans were covered with mud, and her shoes squished when she walked. "I'd better take a bath before Mom sees me," she said. "You wait right here, dog."

The dog wagged his tail as if he understood.

Belinda bathed quickly and put on clean clothes. She was tying her shoes when she heard her father open the front door.

Belinda ran to meet him and exclaimed, "Did you see him?"

"See whom?" Mr. Bean asked.

"The dog!" Belinda cried, running to the door. But there was no dog waiting on the front lawn. She ran to the backyard, but there was no dog there. Belinda sat down on the back steps, wondering sadly where the dog could have gone.

Just then the back door flew open, and her mom and dad came rushing out. "Have you seen Georgie?" her mother cried. "I put him down for his nap a few minutes ago, but he's not in bed now. I can't find him anywhere!"

"Gosh, no, Mom!" Belinda answered. "But

look! My fishing pole is gone, too!"

"The pond!" gasped Mrs. Bean. "Georgie's gone to the pond!"

They dashed down the path. Belinda ran faster than she had ever before in her life. It would be terrible if anything had happened to Georgie.

"Look!" shouted Mr. Bean, stopping suddenly. "Would you look at that?"

Belinda and her mother looked. There, at the edge of the deep pond, was Georgie. He had Belinda's fishing pole clutched tightly in one chubby hand. And right behind Georgie, holding Georgie's shirt tightly with his teeth, was the dog.

"Go 'way, bad doggie," Georgie ordered, struggling to get away.

But the dog didn't let go until Mrs. Bean ran and picked Georgie up.

"Georgie go fishing," Georgie said proudly. Then he frowned and pointed to the dog. "Bad doggie!"

"No, Georgie," said Mrs. Bean. "He's a very good dog, but you've been a naughty boy!"

The dog wagged his tail happily as Belinda and her father stooped to pat his shiny head.

Then Mr. Bean stood and whispered something into Mrs. Bean's ear. She nodded and smiled.

"I'd say every family could use a dog like this one," Mr. Bean said.

"Yes, indeed!" added Mrs. Bean. "Why, he's a real hero!"

"Oh, boy!" shouted Belinda. "And I'm going to call him Hero!"